HARPER
AND THE
Circus of Dreams

For those who love stories, Amelie,
Delphi and Logi – keep the magic. Xxx
C.B.

For a brilliant musician and super duper Grandad
John! Love you lots, big hugs from Twiglett xxx
L.E.A.

First published in the UK in 2016 by Scholastic Children's Books
An imprint of Scholastic Ltd
Euston House, 24 Eversholt Street,
London, NW1 1DB, UK
Registered office: Westfield Road, Southam, Warwickshire, CV47 0RA
SCHOLASTIC and associated logos are trademarks and / or registered
trademarks of Scholastic Inc.

Text copyright © Cerrie Burnell, 2016
Illustrations copyright © Laura Ellen Anderson, 2016

The right of Cerrie Burnell to be identified as the author and
of Laura Ellen Anderson to be identified as the illustrator
has been asserted by them.

HB ISBN 978 1407 15740 5
PB ISBN 978 1407 16607 0

A CIP catalogue record for this book is available from the British Library.

Printed and bound by CPI Group (UK) Ltd, Croydon, CR0 4YY

Papers used by Scholastic Children's Books are made
from wood grown in sustainable forests.

1 3 5 7 9 10 8 6 4 2

www.scholastic.co.uk

HARPER
AND THE
Circus of Dreams

CERRIE BURNELL
Illustrated by Laura Ellen Anderson

■SCHOLASTIC

Once there was a girl called Harper who had a rare musical gift. She heard songs on the wind, rhythms on the rain and hope in the beat of a butterfly's wing. Harper could play every instrument she ever picked up, without learning a single note. Sometimes at night as she drifted to sleep, Harper heard a melody echo down from the stars. But when morning came she could never quite remember the tune. It was the only song she couldn't play – the song that haunted all of her dreams.

Chapter One
A HOWLING WOLF

From the rooftop of the Tall Apartment
Block, Harper perched beneath her Scarlet
Umbrella and gazed down at the City of
Clouds. Sea-Mist rain filled the air, and
twilight swept across the sky, turning the
raindrops the colour of smoke. Everything
was peaceful.

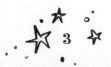

Her beloved cat, Midnight, purred around her ankles, his green eyes twinkling. Harper raised her bow and began to softly play her viola. A single hopeful note rang out before a fierce howling filled the air. Harper dropped her bow and stared around her. There, at the other end of the rooftop, was a wolf the colour of dusk, and a boy lurking in the shadows.

Most children would be terrified of seeing a wolf on their roof. Most children would run and scream with fear. But most children weren't best friends with Nate Nathanielson.

Nate was a boy who lived on the tenth floor. He had found the wolf as a cub, given her a home and named her Smoke.

Smoke loved Nate as if they were part of a pack, and her star-bright eyes could see all the things that Nate could not. She wasn't a guide dog, or a guard dog, or a creature you could you call a pet. She was a wild companion, with wisdom in her heart and the full moon in her howl. But tonight something seemed to be troubling her.

Harper lifted her bow and played three sharp notes – the secret signal to summon her friends. There was a stirring of leaves and a pattering of light feet as a small, mouse-like girl flitted across the roof and threw her arms around the wolf.

"Hello, Liesel," Harper said with a smile, ruffling the small girl's knotted hair.

Liesel, who had large eyes and a love of fairy-tale witches, buried her face in the wolf's silvery coat, trying to soothe her.

The sound of serious footsteps echoed across the roof. "Hi, Ferdie," called Nate, recognizing the sound of his friend's footfall. Ferdie — Liesel's older brother — came hurrying over, still scribbling the last line of a poem. He tightened his scarf, tucked his pencil behind his ear and said, in a serious voice, "I think Smoke's howling at something in the sky."

The others squinted up. Yet all they saw were thickening clouds and the glint of evening starlight.

"It's too dark," moaned Liesel.

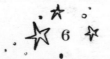

Harper gave her a smile. "What we need," she beamed, "is to fly!"

The children sprang into action. Nate pulled a strand of edentwine from his pocket and fastened Midnight's cat basket to the Scarlet Umbrella's handle. With a wild-eyed grin, Liesel shot into the basket. Ferdie grabbed a strand of twine and attached a big wooden kite to the umbrella's spike, then wove his arms through the kite's bars like a hang-glider. Harper winked at Midnight, who jumped on to her head, landing like a little furry hat. Nate gave a low whistle and, with a breathtaking bound, Smoke pounced on the umbrella's scarlet dome.

Harper and Nate both clasped the

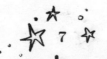

umbrella's handle closely. "Ready?" Harper whispered.

"Ready!" the others called.

"Up!" she cried, and the Scarlet Umbrella soared into the sky, taking the four children, the cat and the wolf with it. The flickering lights of the City of Clouds vanished far below, and the children held their breath as they sailed towards the moon.

Up and up they raced, as if they were lighter than autumn leaves. Liesel leaned out of the cat basket and gave a shriek of joy. The inky sky made her feel like dancing. Ferdie laughed as the Scarlet Umbrella dipped through a fog of silken cloud, his mind filling with a million

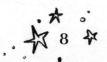

stories. Nate was silent, straining to hear what his wolf might have sensed, and feeling the world shift around him.

Harper kept her eyes closed, for beyond the howl of the wolf and the purr of her cat, she thought she heard music. Just for a moment her heart seemed to tremble, for there was the tune that haunted her dreams – the one she could never quite play. Then they swirled upwards and the song vanished, leaving the world strangely still.

The umbrella hung in darkness, like a red boat on a deep and silent sea. Liesel coughed and giggled, Ferdie fiddled with his scarf, and Harper wondered what sort of cloud this might be, for it didn't look

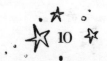

like any of the ones that usually floated above the city. Nate carefully uncurled one hand and ran his fingers through the rain. "There's a storm coming," he whispered.

"A storm?" asked Harper, taking in the stillness of the deep night sky.

Nate shrugged. "Yes. There's something stirring up the wind, mixing everything together. I can feel it."

"But what?" pondered Ferdie, reaching out to touch a drop of moonlight.

Something shot past Liesel like a dart of ice and feathers, and she gave a sudden gasp. "There's someone in the clouds," she squealed. "A ghost in the fog!"

None of the children really believed in

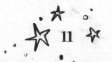

ghosts, yet as they craned their eyes into the dark they saw a girl moving faster than lightning. A girl who seemed to be running on air.

Chapter Two
THE STORY OF THE FEARSOME STORM

"What is it?" asked Nate, who could sense the amazement that gripped his friends.

The others did their best to describe what they could see. "Somewhere within the mist is a girl in a cloak of snow," began Ferdie.

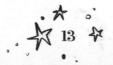

"Her skin is golden brown," said Harper as she watched the girl leap between clouds as easily if they were stepping stones.

"She's got plaits that are full of lightning," piped up Liesel, who was now balancing on top of the cat basket on one foot, trying to get a better look at this wondrous cloud-skipping girl.

Nate opened his mouth to say something, but at that moment thunder bellowed like a bear, and the Scarlet Umbrella was thrown across the sky.

"Hold on!" cried Harper as a whirl of wind that sang like birds whooshed past, filling their heads with harmonies.

"We need to turn the umbrella over," shouted Nate as the singing grew louder.

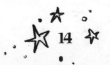

No sooner had Nate spoken than the umbrella spun upside down by itself, catching Harper, Midnight and Nate, and somehow tipping in the wolf too. Ferdie and Liesel screamed as the kite and cat basket collided, and then their mouths fell open as a rainbow of night colours appeared before them. It was the strangest storm the children had ever seen.

Harper gathered her thoughts and, ignoring the song of the storm, she commanded the umbrella to return to the Tall Apartment Block.

As they scrambled back on to the roof Liesel gave a little yelp. "Look at the Scarlet Umbrella," she cried, pointing to

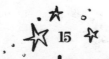

a glistening row of icicles that hung from its bright-red edge.

"And Smoke's fur is full of stars," grinned Nate, putting the tiny glittering fragments carefully in his pocket.

"Midnight's covered in tufts of winter sky," giggled Harper.

"What a super storm," sighed Ferdie, "but who on earth is the girl in the sky?"

"And why could we hear birds singing?" wondered Harper, removing a feather that was caught behind Nate's ear.

"Can we keep the girl in the sky a secret?" Liesel begged.

The children nodded gleefully. For there was nothing more exciting than a secret shared.

The residents of the Tall Apartment Block came hurrying over to help untangle the edentwine. "We haven't seen a storm as good as this for at least five years!" said Elsie Caraham merrily. Elsie was the oldest resident of the Tall Apartment Block and she remembered everything.

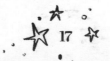

"The skies haven't been so alive since the night of the Fearsome Storm," agreed Harper's Great Aunt Sassy.

Everyone smiled, including Harper. She knew exactly why the Fearsome Storm was special and she loved hearing the tale. "Tell us the story again, Great Aunt Sassy," Harper pleaded as they made their way indoors.

When everyone was gathered inside Harper and Great Aunt Sassy's little flat with a mug of hot cocoa, Sassy began the story. "Five years ago, on the night of the Fearsome Storm, a little girl with dark hair and sea-grey eyes appeared on the rooftop."

"Wow," breathed Liesel, who loved

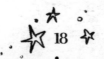

the mystery that surrounded Harper's arrival, and wished with all her heart it had happened to her.

"A little girl clasping a Scarlet Umbrella," added Isabella, a member of the Lucas family from the seventh floor.

"Nobody knew where she'd come from, or how she'd ended up on the roof," said Peter, Ferdie and Liesel's father. "The only clue was a letter, which was pinned to the Scarlet Umbrella by the feather of a dove."

"What did the note say?" asked Ferdie, who knew the answer already but wanted to hear it again.

Great Aunt Sassy swept across the flat and opened a little drawer. Carefully, she

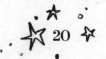

pulled out a crumpled piece of paper, winked warmly at Harper and read the note.

Dearest Aunt Sassy,

This is our beloved daughter, Harper.
Please take great care of her.
We love her more than the dawn
loves the sun or the night adores
the moon.

When the time is right, give her
the Scarlet Umbrella and the
~~Eric~~

All our love,
        Hugo and Aurelia

Nobody knew what the last word said as it had been smudged by a raindrop.

"I hadn't seen my nephew Hugo since he was seven," Sassy explained. "But when I peeked at the small girl beneath the Scarlet Umbrella, my heart fluttered with love. For she had the same sea-grey eyes as me, and I knew at once she belonged here.

Everyone in the little flat grinned and sipped their cocoa. For it was true, Harper and Sassy had been wonderfully happy ever since, living in an apartment block of music and costumes and stories and cats.

Sometimes late at night, it was true that Harper wondered who her parents were, or where they might be. But with

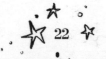

Midnight to keep her company and the residents of the Tall Apartment Block watching over her, she rarely felt sad about it. It was only when she heard her star-song that thoughts of her family danced across her dreams, with a sadness she couldn't quite shake.

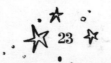

Chapter Three
THE STORM-STIRRER

The next morning Harper awoke to a most unusual sight. A thick white mist had covered the entire city! *How strange*, Harper thought. *It's as if the city has become its name. It really is full of cloud!*

The city got its name from the many different clouds that soared across its sky.

Harper knew most of them by heart, but her favourite ones were:

Star-stealer – a thick black cloud that blots out stars.

Feather-fern – a pale, thin cloud as light as feathers.

Dragonsmoke – a puffy blue cloud seen mostly at twilight.

Snowdrift – endless white clouds as soft as snow.

Great Aunt Sassy burst into the kitchen and flung her suitcase down in despair. "The Dutch Opera House are sending a helicopter to collect me," she wailed, "but they'll never find the

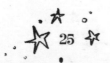

Tall Apartment Block in all this fog."

Midnight leaped from the window sill and vanished into the hallway. With a light flick of his tail he opened the Scarlet Umbrella and tugged it over to Harper. She stared at the rich red fabric and smiled. "It's OK, Great Aunt Sassy," she laughed. "The scarlet silk will show up in the mist. We can use the umbrella as a beacon."

Ten minutes later Nate had attached the Scarlet Umbrella firmly to the rooftop by edentwine. "There is no way the wind can blow you away," he said proudly, "and if the storm starts up again, give three sharp tugs and we'll pull you back down."

Harper sat down deep in the umbrella's

folds, and wrapped her arms around Midnight.

"Keep a lookout for the girl in the sky," muttered Nate. "See if you can find out who she is."

"I will," Harper murmured, closing her eyes and sending the umbrella up to a Snowdrift sky.

When the edentwine stretched taut, Harper raised Elsie Caraham's spyglass to her eye and peered around. All she could see for miles and miles were clouds that glistened like snow. She pulled her piccolo flute from her pocket and played a song of myths and mountains, a melody of magical ice. As her fingers found the notes, a little breeze picked up, tickling

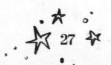

27

Midnight's tail.

Then came the sound of beating wings.

Harper froze as two white-winged eagles broke through the a Feather-fern cloud. They were the hugest birds she had ever seen – like kings of the sky. Behind them soared a flight of other stormy birds, who were beautiful and fierce all at once. The birds circled them in a swirl of song,

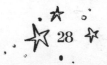

and from within them stepped a girl in a cloak of pale feathers – the girl who could run on air.

The girl stood tall like a queen amongst her flock. She sang a soft note and the birds dived right. She roared like thunder and the birds arched left. She called like a swallow and the birds seemed to hang in the air without moving. Harper was too stunned to speak.

As the girl came nearer, running across the sky, Harper noticed a tightrope, thin and silvery, reaching through the mist. She peeked through the spyglass and found that the sky was full of tightropes, each end tethered loosely to the neck of a great storm-coloured bird.

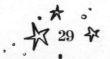

29

"What's your name?" asked Harper in a voice as soft as breath.

"I'm Skylar," sang the girl, diving on to the back of a white-winged eagle.

"Where did you learn to run on tightropes?" Harper asked.

"I grew up in a circus," Skylar smiled. "We travel the world by wind. My job is to mix up the weather. I'm a storm-stirrer."

Harper's eyes opened wide with astonishment. "So that's what you were doing last night, and that's why the wind sang like birds."

Skylar nodded. "I stir a mighty storm so the Circus of Dreams can arrive in secret."

Harper leaned out of the Scarlet Umbrella. "What's the Circus of Dreams?"

"It's a circus bound by spells. You must come. We're in the far north of the city. But be quick... When the wind changes, we leave." And with that, the white-winged bird swooped away, taking the storm-stirrer with it.

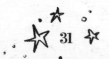

The sound of a propeller thrummed through the mist. Harper waved a wild hello to the Dutch Opera House pilot, and then tugged happily on the twine, staring at the far-off wings of the eagles as she glided back to the Tall Apartment Block.

As soon as the helicopter had landed and Harper was safely on the roof, she played three sharp notes on her piccolo flute. "I know who the girl in the sky is!" she cried as her three best friends gathered around her. "She's a storm-stirrer! She belongs to a circus that travels by wind."

"A storm-stirrer," gasped Ferdie, his mind imagining a glorious poem.

"A queen of wild weather," squealed Liesel.

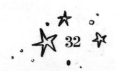

32

"A circus that travels by wind," said Nate, his face glowing with smiles.

The children were still for a moment, the same bright thought glittering in each of their minds. "We have to go to the circus!" yelled Liesel.

"Yes," said Harper, "and we will!"

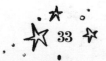

Chapter Four
MUSIC IN THE MIST

As the helicopter rose into the sky, Great Aunt Sassy waved a velvet glove through the mist and called a fond goodbye. She was off with the Dutch Opera House for a weekend in Holland, while Harper was staying with Madame Flora at the ballet school on floor three.

"Let's split up and find someone to take us to the circus," said Ferdie eagerly.

The children nodded and scampered away. Harper knocked on the ballet school door, but Madame Flora gently shook her head – she was teaching classes all day.

Ferdie and Liesel raced home to their flat on floor five. But their father, Peter, a famous German writer, only muttered about having to finish his next novel. Brigitte, their mother, was halfway through painting a portrait of Ludo the cat.

Nate's mum was at the library, and his two older brothers were fixing a broken guitar, so he tried the Lucas family on floor seven, only to find them having a party for the twins' birthday.

The last person left to ask was wise old Elsie Caraham.

"Oh, Harper," Elsie sighed, "I would love nothing more than to visit that extraordinary circus. But I have to look after Memphis and Tallulah's kittens."

Harper knelt to stroke the little bundles of fur and tails. A kitten with silver and black stripes whipped out a claw and scratched her. Harper didn't mind at all.

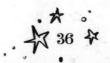

If there was one thing she loved it was cats.

Elsie tutted. "That kitten's a little bit wild," she mumbled as she waved Harper away.

Harper wandered out of Elsie's flat and went to find the others. They were perched on the rooftop, looking down at the sleek white streets below.

"We've never crossed the city alone by foot," said Harper.

"And the trams won't run in the mist," said Ferdie.

Liesel kicked a plant pot. She was feeling very cross indeed. "If only I were a mouse," she grumbled, "then my nose would lead us to the Circus of Dreams."

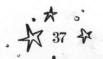

"We just need to wait until the mist clears," Harper said soothingly. "Then I can fly us there in the Scarlet Umbrella."

Nate put his head on one side. "Maybe we don't need to wait," he shrugged. "Maybe I can lead us there. I can find my way around in the dark, so the mist shouldn't be that different."

The others clapped their hands in delight. Though Nate couldn't make out his friends' faces, he felt the warmth of their gaze, and he grinned at them. "Come on! Let's do it!"

"What if we lose sight of you?" asked Ferdie. "It will be like we're wandering through Star-stealer cloud."

"Instruments!" yelled Liesel. "If we all

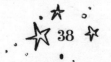

play the same song, we can follow the sound."

Everyone nodded and Smoke gave a yelp of agreement, shaking her fur and scattering stars. The children quickly picked them up and wove them into their hair. They looked quite wonderful, as if they'd been sprinkled with moon dust. "Goodbye," they called to the other residents as they clattered down the stairs, promising to bring back stories from the circus.

As afternoon shadows fell across the city, four proud figures emerged through the murky mist, each of them edged with the glow of fallen stars. First came a boy with a golden-eyed wolf. Upon his head – over his pork-pie cap – was

a trusty tambourine, and in his arms he carried a bronze trumpet he'd just started learning.

He was followed closely by a girl as nimble as a little brown mouse. In one hand Liesel held a bow, in the other, her gleaming violin. Behind her came Ferdie with his squeaky button accordion gripped tightly to his chest.

Lastly came the girl with the rare musical gift. Harper could have played any instrument, although she'd never really known which one was truly for her. This time, Harper had chosen Great Aunt Sassy's Mexican banjo.

Three paces behind the line of children tiptoed Midnight, his white-tipped tail

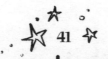

almost invisible in the frosty mist. Harper cleared her throat and called out a count of four, and they all began to play.

As they wove through the empty streets, Nate and Harper kept the main tune going, a folk song of fairy tales. Liesel played the harmony, and Ferdie added off-key chords that sighed. *This mist is nothing at all like cloud,* Harper thought. *It's full of marvels and mystery.*

Crossing the city was no easy task. It was a huge jumble of streets, lined with museums and cafes and birdhouses. It normally rained every single day, in many different ways. But the mist had stolen away the rain, leaving the air feeling cold and crisp.

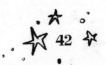

Nate followed the deserted tram tracks until the scent of lilacs filled his nose. "We're at the Museum of Flowers!" he yelled, honking loudly on his trumpet.

A few steps later, Smoke gave a sudden growl and Nate paused, bending down to feel the ground around him. It was soft and mossy like the bank of a river Nate pulled a star from his pocket and dropped it, listening to the sound of it splash as it fell. They had reached a small, dark canal. Carefully Smoke guided the children alongside it. Then the air was alive with the twitter of birds. "The Central Aviary," Nate said with a grin. "We're halfway there."

On they stumbled, down a street lined

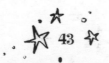

with pancake houses and across a leafy park. Somewhere along the journey Midnight wandered away. But Harper wasn't worried. Midnight knew the city as well as he knew his own whiskers.

As the mist thinned everyone stopped still. Above them was something that seemed to have fallen from a dream. The unmistakable red-and-gold of a circus tent, only this one was floating high in the clouds.

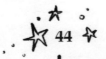

Chapter Five
THE RED-AND-GOLD TENT

The first time you see magic, you will feel
it in your heart and know it in your toes.
The air around you will thicken and the
world will seem to glitter. Nothing else
will matter but the wonder of impossible
things coming true. This was how the
children felt as they stared at the red-and-

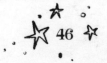

gold tent. Harper could not stop beaming, for the circus seemed so familiar, like she had seen it before, long ago.

"How does it stay afloat?" gasped Ferdie, ignoring the urge to reach for his pencil and start scribbling a thousand stories.

"I don't care how," yelled Liesel, who knew that something extraordinary was happening and felt her heart soar with joy.

Nate sensed the splendour of the tent above, and Smoke, for once, was perfectly still.

"Hot-air balloons!" said Ferdie suddenly.

Harper and Liesel saw that Ferdie was right. The red-and-gold tent was held in the air by a huge indigo balloon. Behind it was a carnival of other bright tents, all

hanging from colourful balloons, towed through the sky by birds.

"Look! That's the way in," shrieked Liesel, pointing to a rope ladder that dropped down from the tent.

The children tucked their instruments away and hurried to join the queue. The moment Liesel put her foot on the ladder's rungs she felt a sense of enchantment tickle her feet, and she darted up the rungs as quick as a mouse. Ferdie climbed fast behind her, his scarf seriously billowing, his eyes wide open with wonder.

Harper flipped the Scarlet Umbrella open and spun it upside down. "Meet us at the top!" she said to Nate, helping him and Smoke climb in. With a little

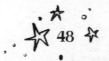

tap she sent the umbrella sailing towards the clouds. Then she placed her feet on the rungs and stepped towards the sky.

Though the ladder was light and thin, it was safe and easy to climb. The City of Clouds spread out below, and Harper saw that everywhere, apart from the park, was still cloaked with mist. The scent of woodsmoke and toffee apples came drifting down and Harper paused.

"Perhaps I visited this circus when I was small," she murmured, "or perhaps I came here in my dreams." For even though it was new and exciting, something about it also felt like home.

"Come on, I want to go in!" screamed Liesel, who had reached the top and was

going wild. Ferdie scrambled up after her and held the umbrella steady for Nate to climb out.

"I think we're standing on solid Dragonsmoke," said Nate, inspecting the ground beneath his feet.

Liesel dropped to her knees and nibbled the cloud. "No, it's bitter candyfloss," she laughed.

"Ready?" said Harper. "Let's go in!"

Together they stepped into the red-and-gold tent, and into a new adventure.

Chapter Six
THE LIGHTNING-LEADER

The inside of the tent was made entirely of black velvet. On a throne of silver in the centre sat an old and startlingly elegant woman who, just like Skylar the storm-stirrer, had lightning in her hair. "How many tickets would you like?" she asked.

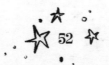

The children fidgeted. No one had thought to bring any money.

The woman with lightning hair seemed to read their minds. "Never mind," she said kindly. "I believe you know my great granddaughter, Skylar." They all nodded happily. "So perhaps you can just give me something precious instead."

"Are you a storm-stirrer too?" whispered Liesel, who was so struck with awe she was almost speechless.

The woman's brown eyes twinkled and her silver-grey afro crackled with blue light. "I'm a lightning-leader," she explained. "I stop the storm once the circus has arrived. There's only ever been one storm I couldn't tame."

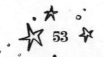

"Which one?" asked Ferdie, his mind dancing with words.

The lightning-leader shook her head almost sadly. "Why, the Fearsome Storm, of course," she replied.

Everyone was quiet. In the velvety darkness Nate reached for Harper's hand. "That's a very special storm to us," Harper

murmured. The lightning-leader nodded, and studied Harper's face for a moment before beckoning Ferdie to come forward.

Ferdie fumbled in his pocket and pulled out a handful of poems. "Will one of these do as a ticket?" he asked brightly.

The lightning-leader sat taller on her throne and considered it, and then she took a single sentence from the middle of the poem, plucking the pencil letters right off the page and turning them into smoke.

The children gasped and Liesel stepped up, hoping the lightning-leader might turn her into a mouse or a wicked spider, but the lightning-leader simply reached out a slender hand and lifted a drop of rain from Liesel's tangled hair.

Next Harper played a melody of miracles on the Mexican banjo whilst the lightning-leader just gazed at her oddly.

Nate played a tremendous trumpet solo, while Smoke shook the tambourine in her teeth. The lightning-leader laughed softly and pinched a strand of fur from Smoke's silvery coat.

"You may pass," she announced, peeling open the curtains. The four children and the wolf thanked her and darted into the Circus of Dreams.

An entire city of little tents bobbed before them, each pitched upon a candyfloss cloud. The tents were every colour you could imagine — and some you could not. They were held in place

by hot-air balloons and linked together by sugary bridges that were as thin and wiry as cobwebs. "What shall we see first?" cried Liesel, feeling her feet suddenly drawn towards a stripy tent.

"Whatever you wish," smiled Harper.

"We could split up and try to find the storm-stirrer?" suggested Nate.

"Whoever finds her first play three sharp notes," said Ferdie. "Music is our secret signal!" The children waved goodbye and set off through the floating circus.

Chapter Seven
THE CIRCUS OF DREAMS

Ferdie strode across a candyfloss bridge towards a tent that smelled like Paris. Inside he found a cake shop like none he had ever seen. Chocolate eclairs were sculpted into the shape of glass slippers. Marzipan mice had jelly-bean hearts that seemed to beat in their tiny chests. And a

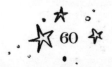

miniature library of books had been carved out of gingerbread.

"Go ahead, have a nibble – everything's free," came a friendly voice.

Ferdie looked up to see a tall baker in a sweeping black apron. His long hair and beard were the blackish grey of storm clouds, but his eyes were warm and kind.

Ferdie took a bite of a book. "That's incredible," he stuttered, for instead of tasting gingerbread, he heard the lines of a story inside his head. It wasn't just any old sentence, but the very same one the lightning-leader had taken as a ticket. "What else shall I try?" Ferdie asked.

"One of these," said the storm-cloud

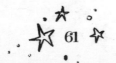

baker, offering him a biscuit shaped like a harp. To Ferdie's delight, it filled his mind with music. The tune was dreamy and starry and made him think of summer moons. Next he sipped sweet tea from a cup made entirely of cake. The tea tasted of strawberries, and with the taste came a memory.

All at once Ferdie was lost in his thoughts, remembering his seventh birthday when Liesel had stolen Elsie Caraham's prize strawberries to give him as a gift. So he didn't see the storm-cloud baker open a dark umbrella and fly to the top of the tent to fetch some lemon curd. Nor did he see him sail down again and tuck the umbrella under the counter. Instead,

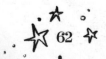

Ferdie stood completely still, enchanted by the memory of strawberries. Then he thanked the storm-cloud baker, waved a serious wave, and hurried on to explore the next tent.

On the other side of the circus, Harper was halfway across a swaying pink bridge when she heard the same tune she had played for her ticket. She skipped after it into a tiny tepee draped with flowers. There, in the middle, curled upon a silken cushion, was her Midnight.

"There you are!" Harper laughed, hugging her cat tightly. You see, Midnight was a most unusual cat. He had a way of knowing exactly where Harper was going to be, long before she arrived. Nobody ever knew how he did it.

"Come in, come in," came a crackly voice. Harper saw a little old woman with crimson lips and nightshade curls perched

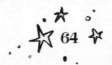

on a stool at the back. "She looks like a character from one of Great Aunt Sassy's operas," Harper whispered to Midnight, who gave a meow of agreement.

"I'm Faydra, teller of fortunes," the woman cackled. "Ask me a question and I shall find you an answer."

Harper thought for a moment. She would have loved to ask about her parents – where they might be, what they were like. But she didn't quite dare to. So instead she asked, "Which instrument is truly for me?"

Faydra glared at a shiny crystal ball and mumbled, "Listen, Harper, you must play the instrument that quiets a storm. That is the only way."

Harper didn't understand what that meant, but she thanked Faydra all the same, popped Midnight on to her shoulder, and wandered away to discover what lay in the next wonderful tent.

On the furthest cloud from Harper, Nate and Smoke were taking their time, feeling the strangeness of the spun-sugar bridges and breathing the smells of woodsmoke and toffee.

Smoke stopped, her ears pricked to the wind. Nate crouched beside her and listened. Slowly, a song came calling to him. A song of sea light and frozen tides, as if

the singer was deep underwater. It was the most haunting melody Nate had ever heard.

"Follow the song," he whispered to Smoke and he kept his hand on her back as she strolled into a crowded tent. Nate couldn't quite make out what colour the tent was, but he supposed it was mystical turquoise.

Inside it was packed. There was a rush of air above him and, from the top of the tent, Nate saw a silvery shadow swing into the light. A woman on a trapeze, he guessed, only she was swinging in and out of a pool of clear water, her song never faltering. Nate imagined her to be beautiful, like a mermaid acrobat with eyes the colour of the sea. And he was right,

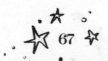

for her eyes were a wintery sea-grey and filled with a look of sadness.

At the end of the song as she dived from her trapeze and into the water, she searched the crowd as if she was seeking someone out. But Nate was too far to feel her gaze, and the tent was too crowded for Smoke to see that around her neck the sea-singer wore a garland of feathers and fur – fur plucked from the coat of a silver wolf.

A little way off Liesel stood outside a stripy tent, staring at a sign that read: THE DAZZLING RAT DANCERS. She had never seen a rat before. The City of Clouds had once been overrun by them,

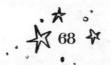

which was why every household now
had a cat, but that had been long before
she was born.

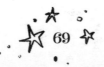

She crept inside, her heart beating with hope, but the tent was empty. Liesel stared as a boy stepped out of the darkness and on to a fine tightrope. He was tall with narrow eyes and slightly pointed teeth. On a string around his neck he wore the same glistening raindrop that had been pulled from Liesel's hair. She watched curiously as the boy began to play a melodeon. The instrument crumpled and sagged in his hands, and the boy seemed half asleep, even when nine enormous white rats came scampering forward. The rats were so nimble and quick, it was like watching miniature ballerinas. It was beautiful, but also quite boring.

Liesel was very disappointed. "Your rats

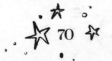

70

are very dull," she called. "They don't even look wicked!"

The boy snarled angrily, showing teeth that were like those of a rat.

"What makes you think rats are wicked?" he snapped, walking on his hands up and down the tightrope.

Liesel tried to hide how impressed she was. "It says so in all the fairy tales," she shrugged.

"Not my rats," said the boy said as he hung upside down by his knees. "I trained them myself. Watch this!"

He began to play the melodeon again, only this time the tune was a merry muddle of madness, sending the rats into a series of flips and tricks. The boy turned

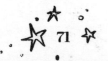

a somersault and landed on his knees at
Liesel's feet, a trail of white rats spinning
behind him.

Liesel clapped until her hands hurt.
"Why don't you play that song in your
show?"

The boy chuckled sadly. "I want to, but my uncle won't let me. He's the ringmaster, Othello Grande. He controls the entire circus."

Liesel blinked and held out her hand, deciding that she liked this bedraggled rat boy. "I'm Liesel," she said boldly. "I'm sorry your uncle's so strict."

The boy shook her hand roughly. "I'm Rat," he said with a vermin-like grin. "It's OK. When the curtains are closed we do the tricks we want to do, anyway."

Liesel's eyes brightened. "When can I see that show?" she asked.

Rat sniffed the air and twitched his ears. "Just about now," he answered. "Follow

me." And just like that, a friendship began between a girl who longed to be a mouse, and a boy who looked like a rat.

They climbed up a series of ladders to the heavens of the circus. When they reached the top Liesel's mouth fell open, for before them was a company of wild circus kids, and amongst them stood Skylar the storm-stirrer. Liesel grabbed her violin and played three sharp notes.

Chapter Eight
THE CHILDREN OF THE CIRCUS

To Liesel's amazement there wasn't just one storm-stirrer, but a whole troupe rehearsing in the heavens of the circus – a landscape of hot-air balloons that bobbed like silky moons. She scrambled after Rat to the very top of a huge indigo balloon to watch a display of cartwheels and acrobatics.

A small pink dove flew into her hair, mistaking it for a nest, and Liesel giggled, tucking her violin safely away and cupping the bird in her hands.

A flash of a white-tipped tail caught Liesel's eye, as Midnight strolled across a balloon. She waved as Harper, Nate, Smoke and Ferdie appeared at the top of the ladder. The performing children stilled their rehearsal and stared cautiously at the wolf. They were afraid of seeing such a fierce creature so close, and without a lead.

The air was so still it felt solid, but Harper knew what to do. She picked up her Mexican banjo and played a few bars of a lively tune. Ferdie followed on the

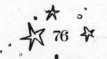

button accordion, and Nate started tooting on the trumpet.

Liesel jumped up and began pirouetting around the wolf, her feet as fast as raindrops. Smoke howled and, with a sudden bound, raced in a ring around the heavens of the circus, her fur still dappled with stars, making her look like a firework. The storm-stirrers cheered.

Rat added a new melody on the melodeon and Skylar began to sing. Birds came dipping and diving from the sky in a stunning storm of falling feathers. For a moment every child smiled, the music binding them together with the promise of new friendships.

When the song finished all the

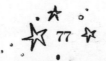

circus kids gathered around the wolf in amazement, and Nate told them the wonderful story of how he had found her as a pup, mistaken her for a dog, and brought her home.

A girl with freckles whose name was Sunbeam scooped up Midnight. "Tell us another story," she murmured, so Harper told them about the night of Midnight's arrival and the way he had simply turned up to her little flat at the stroke of twelve and never left. The name had seemed perfect.

"We don't have any cats up in the sky," said Sunbeam.

"Well, you must come to the City of Clouds," cried Ferdie. "It's full of cats!

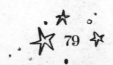

That's why the birds live in birdhouses, to keep them safe from hunting cats"

"Our birds are tethered to us, but they fly freely," said Skylar, "towing the circus, chasing the wind."

"Nobody – not even Othello Grande – knows where the circus is headed," said Rat.

The children gasped, and Sunbeam whispered, "And if you are born into the circus you are bound by magic and can never leave."

The storm-stirrers all nodded in agreement. "There has only ever been one child who got out," said Skylar, "and nobody knows how. Except that it happened in the midst of a storm."

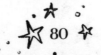

Nate, Ferdie, Harper and Liesel could have sat there all day, listening to the secrets of the circus, but at that moment a siren sounded and the storm-stirrers all sprang gracefully to their feet.

"That's the call for dinner," yelled Skylar as she dived on to the back of a white-winged eagle. "We've got to go, but come and see us again soon!" Then she was gone, and the four children, the cat and the wolf found themselves alone on the silken balloon.

It was only Nate who noticed that the hot-air balloon didn't feel hot or airy at all. It felt strong and trustworthy and very similar to something he knew well, only he couldn't think what.

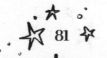

"Do we have to go home?" sighed Liesel, who could quite easily have run away with the circus.

"I suppose we do," said Ferdie, "but we can always come back tomorrow."

They cheered up at this thought and went skipping back through the snow-white city, taking turns to play their instruments, the smiles on their faces glittering through the mist brighter than the stars they wore in their hair.

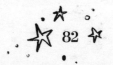

Chapter Nine
HARPER'S NOTE

When they reached the Tall Apartment Block, Harper headed straight for the ballet school on the third floor. She found Madame Flora with Isabella Lucas and Snowflake, the ballet school cat, all busily practising their pas de chats.

"The circus was magical," Harper

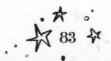

sighed, describing the many floating tents.

Isabella clapped her hand to her heart. "How long is the circus in town?" she cried, fluttering the wings of her costume like a butterfly.

"Nobody knows," Harper whispered. "It moves on when the wind changes."

"I must go at once," Isabella cried, throwing a colourful shawl around her shoulders and flying out of the door.

"I visited the Circus of Dreams long ago," said Madame Flora with a faraway look in her eye. "I sipped a sweet tea that tasted of memories and I heard a woman singing underwater." As she spoke she rose on to perfect points and vanished into her studio flat, returning with a postcard

and a cake wrapper. "These are the two souvenirs I saved from the circus,"

Harper studied them closely. On the front of the postcard was a faded artist's drawing of a beautiful woman on a trapeze, underwater. Next to the drawing were the words *Aurelia: sea-singer.*

Harper held the card very still. Aurelia. She had heard that name somewhere before.

Next she picked up the cake wrapper. It was old and crinkly, and on the back was stamped the logo of a little circus tent. Beneath were the words *Hugo: Baker of Wonder and Wishes.*

Hugo. Harper had heard that name somewhere before too. She stared at

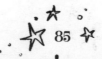

Madame Flora and gulped. "Can you remember when you visited the Circus of Dreams?"

Madame Flora thought for a moment. "Well, it must have been about five years

ago. Around the night of the Fearsome Storm…"

Harper clutched the faded postcard to her chest, and squeezed the crinkly wrapper tight. Then she was on her feet, hammering three sharp notes on the cherry-wood piano, tearing out the door and fleeing up the stairs. Madame Flora had no idea what was going on, all she could do was follow.

Harper ran as if she might never stop, for she had realized something wonderful. Into her little flat she fled, grabbing the note that Great Aunt Sassy had kept safe for her. As her friends piled into the room, she held up the postcard and said in a quivering voice, "The sea-singer from the

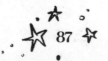

Circus of Dreams is called Aurelia," and then she slowly unfurled her fingers from the cake wrapper. "And the baker from the Circus of Dreams is called Hugo."

The room went very quiet. All Harper could hear was the beat of her heart, loud as thunder. With a trembling finger she pointed to the note. "My parents' names are Hugo and Aurelia," she whispered.

Ferdie, Nate, Liesel and Madame Flora all gave an enormous gasp.

"So your parents are with the Circus of Dreams?" asked Nate in a voice so soft, it was quieter than snow. Harper nodded. "That makes perfect sense," he smiled.

"Why?" asked Ferdie, who was feeling as shocked as Harper.

"Those hot air-balloons that keep the circus afloat," said Nate, "well, I don't think they're balloons at all. I think they're flying umbrellas!"

The whole room began talking excitedly. Madame Flora did an accidental curtsy, Smoke growled, Midnight meowed, Liesel shrieked and Ferdie almost fell over in amazement. "So your Scarlet Umbrella came from the Circus of Dreams," he breathed. "That's why the lightning-leader looked at you so strangely – I think she recognized you."

Liesel's eyes widened with astonishment. "You are the child who escaped the circus!" she cried. "You are the girl from Skylar's story." Harper slowly nodded, as

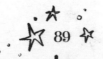

she realized it was true. Liesel stamped her foot crossly. "Why can't anything that exciting happen to me!" she huffed.

Ferdie glared at his sister, but Harper took her hand. "Come back to the circus with me, and help me find them," she stammered.

"Let's all go together," said Madame Flora, plucking a harmonica from her pocket and readying herself to march through the mist.

But no sooner had they stepped on to the stairwell than Isabella Lucas appeared. "Oh, Harper," she said sadly, "I rushed to reach the circus, but it had already left."

Harper felt the Mexican banjo slip from her hands and fall to the floor. She

might have sunk to the ground herself if
Midnight hadn't leaped from the darkness
and landed in her arms. His loud purr was
such a comfort. She hid her face in his
silky black fur, trying to hide her tears.
"I came so close to finding my family,"
she whispered, "but now
I'm too late."

Chapter Ten
THE TERRIFYINGLY TALL MAN

"Too late? Never!" said Ferdie, and he snatched up the Mexican banjo and threw his arm around Harper's shoulder. "Don't worry, Harper – as long as there are clouds in the sky there is hope," he announced in his most poetic voice.

Nate reached through the shadows of

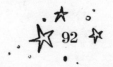

the stairwell and took Harper's hand. "We'll find them, Harper. There must be a way."

Liesel closed her eyes and thought as hard as she could, in her most mouse-like manner. "We need to find someone who knows the circus," she said. "Someone magical."

Nate put his head on one side. "You're right, Liesel," he cried. "We need to find the Wild Conductor!"

Harper wiped away her tears, suddenly feeling much better.

"If there's any way to find a wizard," said Madame Flora wisely, "it's going to be through music." With a swish of her classical tutu she disappeared off to ring the

meeting bell, and ask once again for the help of the residents of the Tall Apartment Block.

As a deep, dark dusk swept across the city, and Cloudburst rain broke from the sky, the residents of the Tall Apartment Block brought a marvellous collection of instruments to the roof. There was the grand cherry-wood piano, an ancient double bass, Ferdie's button accordion, Harper's clarinet, Nate's brother's Roman tuba and a xylophone.

"The last time we saw the Wild Conductor was on the banks of the River North," said Nate as he helped Mariana and Paulo Lucas wind Great Aunt Sassy's sheets into a rope of lavender silk.

"I doubt he'll be there now," said Ferdie, joining his parents as they fastened the rope to each instrument.

Elsie Caraham tied the end of the rope to the Scarlet Umbrella's handle and helped Harper and Nate climb in. Isabella swept them into a hug and murmured, "If the Wild Conductor is still trying to create an orchestra of animals, then he might be at one of the birdhouses."

Harper hugged her back as tightly as she could. "We'll start looking at the Central

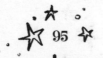

95

Aviary," she said with a smile. Nate gave a shrill whistle and Midnight and Smoke both shot into the umbrella.

"Good luck!" said Ferdie, punching the air.

"Be careful, little Harp," said Peter fondly.

"We'll wait for you right here," cooed Madame Flora.

Liesel was trying very hard not to sulk. She desperately wanted to go and seek the man with the magpie-feather hair. But she knew there just wasn't enough room in the umbrella. She pulled herself together and in her bravest voice said, "Go find the Wild Conductor!"

With a soft *whoosh* the umbrella rose

into the air, a rope of instruments trailing below. Night was falling around them, and Star-stealer clouds darkened the sky.

"Do you remember last summer when you got every cat in the City of Clouds to follow your tune?" asked Nate. Harper nodded. "Maybe we could try the same with birds."

Harper smiled. "All right," she said, carefully climbing over the edge of the Scarlet Umbrella and sliding down the rope of lavender silk, with Midnight close behind.

As the Scarlet Umbrella hovered high above the Central Aviary, Midnight gave a loud *Meow!* and began to play the cherry-wood piano alongside Harper. Harper

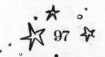

closed her eyes and let the evening lead her to a lullaby of long-forgotten dreams, the sadness of the day and the hope of the future flowing through her fingers into the ivory keys. Softly her tune rained down on the city and the night birds awakened. Two green parakeets stretched out their wings and copied the melody, and a yellow-tailed parrot followed. Then a chorus of owls took up the harmony.

"It's working, keep playing!" cried Nate from the umbrella.

The more Harper played, the more birds joined in, and what a delightful sound they made – a sound that could hit you like an arrow of feathers and make you long to fly.

Nate crouched next to his wolf and stroked her star-tangled fur. "Listen up, girl," he whispered, "keep your eyes out for the Wild Conductor. If you see him, howl like a hurricane!"

Smoke gave a sharp growl – then she peered down across the City of Clouds, her golden eyes like two small candles. A shadow swept through the streets and the wolf bared her teeth. The shadow seemed terrifyingly tall, with a long satin coat darker than night. The wolf's fur bristled. The shadow slunk from a back street to an alleyway, until it was beneath the birdhouse. Moonlight fell on the shadow's face and the wolf howled like a winter wind. Harper jumped and stared

down from the cherry-wood piano. There below her was the man with magpie-feather hair. The Wild Conductor.

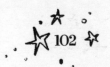

"Good evening," he said in a deep, velvety voice. He was still a little bitter about last summer when Harper had won Midnight back from him, but despite himself he was pleased to see both the children.

"Evening," called Nate as the umbrella drifted slowly down, until the cherry-wood piano was level with the tall man's eyes.

"Remember how you wanted to find the Circus of Dreams?" asked Harper. The

Wild Conductor gave a fierce nod.

"Well, we might be able to help you," cried Nate.

A sad, dark laugh escaped the Wild Conductor's lips. "Impossible!" he said dryly. "You must charm them with a talent or summon them with a skill, or put on a performance that will make their hearts stand still. Not even my talent is enough." Then his face twitched with an idea. "Unless of course you are asking me to reform the cat orchestra?"

The children both smiled. "Well, you did say a cat orchestra could summon a circus across many seas," Harper answered.

The Wild Conductor mulled over his thoughts. "It would have to be something

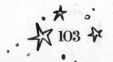

more spectacular than just the cats," he muttered. "It would have to be a fabulous fantasia of fairy tales."

He looked into Harper's sea-grey eyes, and shrugged awkwardly. "Why do you want to find the circus anyway?"

Harper held his gaze and gripped the rope of lavender silk. "I think Aurelia may be my mother," she gulped, "and Hugo my father."

To her surprise the Wild Conductor swept into a low elegant bow and said, "In that case I will help you in any way I can," and for the first time his voice was filled with promise.

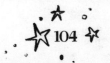

Chapter Eleven
A SPLENDID CONCERT

The next week sped by in a rush of rehearsals and hand-stitched gowns. Great Aunt Sassy returned from Holland and worked late into the night creating a wonderful collection of costumes for the concert. Nate's older brothers built a little stage beneath the canopy of storm blooms.

And all the residents came together to help Harper put on a heart-stopping show.

When the day of the concert finally arrived Harper felt as if an entire flock of butterflies was taking flight in her tummy. She peered at the Wild Conductor, who stood alone at the edge of the roof, his arms out wide as if he were conducting the sky. She stared at the makeshift orchestra pit, where the cat orchestra were curled, rows of tails and teeth, yellow eyes and moon-white claws, each clasping a miniature instrument. Siamese cats were on strings. Tabbies and tortoiseshell took percussion. Sleek black or bright-white cats were on woodwind. Speckled and spotted cats took brass. They were all

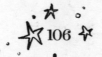

wearing waterproof bonnets that Sassy had stitched, which made Harper want to giggle.

Her eyes came to rest on Midnight. He flicked his ear and twanged his mandolin. Harper rose to her feet. It was time for the show to begin.

Harper took a breath and began to play. As the notes wove their wave into the audience's hearts, Midnight began following on the mandolin. Then Snowflake took up the viola, Katarina, the Lucas family's cat, gave a shake of the samba cowbells, Memphis and Tallulah began squeaking on the bagpipes, and

Ludo, Ferdie and Liesel's cat, thwacked the bass drum with his tail. The Wild Conductor gave a swish of his wand and every cat joined in.

When the music was at a steady pace, Ferdie stepped into the spotlight, a serious boy with a serious scarf. He cleared his throat and read out his newest poem, *Fearsome Storm, We Are Not Afraid*. Then Madame Flora took to the stage to perform the dance of the dying swan, as Elsie Caraham played a soft, sad solo on an old viola.

Next Nate moved into the spotlight, feeling the glow of its warmth on his face. He lit a sparkler and drew a circle of pale fire in the air. Everyone froze

as Smoke emerged from the wings with Liesel clinging to her back. Nate gave a low, long whistle and Smoke dived through the ring of sparks, carrying the small girl with her.

Isabella burst on to the stage, spinning and flittering like a firefly, a crown of tiger lilies shimmering in her hair. Peter and Brigitte leaped to their feet and performed a fast German polka all around the rooftop. Great Aunt Sassy gathered an armful of Spanish fans and did the dance of ducks. A quiet man called Jack Willows, who was the caretaker of the Unforgotten Concert Hall, came forward with a beautiful, strange old harp, and surprised everyone by playing "The Dance of the Sugar Plum Fairy". As Harper watched him pluck the dusty strings, a sense of enchantment gripped her heart. Suddenly she believed that the concert really would work, that she really could summon the Circus of Dreams.

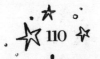

A Heartbeat rain gushed down, and the residents raised teacups and tankards to the sky and swigged the sweet, fresh water. For the finale, as the cat orchestra played on, Harper took up a collection of instruments and began juggling with them, playing each one as it passed through her fingers or sailed past her lips. She didn't miss a single beat. It was a song of midnight rainbows and the poetry of stars. A song of stories yet to be written, and friendships made in the clouds. She played with all she had, her face tipped to the horizon, searching for a red-and-gold tent. Just as the music came to an end, she saw something that made her tremble. A

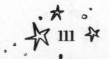

white-winged eagle swooping through the sky. The Circus of Dreams was coming back!

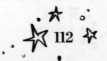

Chapter Twelve
THE DREAM SONG

All at once, lightning split the sky and the cats dropped their instruments and scattered. Thunder Break rain lashed down and the air turned eerie white.

Quickly Sassy and Elsie began hurrying everyone inside. The Wild Conductor stood tall. Ferdie and Liesel took shelter beneath

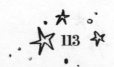

the Scarlet Umbrella, and Midnight dropped his mandolin and ran to Harper's side.

Nate came swishing across the roof with Smoke. "I'll stay with you," he yelled to Harper, reaching out for her hand. Then the girl, the cat, the boy and the wolf turned to face the storm.

Snowflakes danced before their eyes, and they crouched down low, shielding their faces. A mist of marvels and mystery covered the rooftop.

"The circus is coming," whispered Harper, but the mist vanished in front of her eyes, the thunder faded to a dull echo, and sunlight shone through the rain. Just like that, it was over. The storm was gone and the Circus of Dreams was nowhere to be seen. "I don't understand," Harper stammered.

The Wild Conductor fell to his knees. "I'm so sorry," he said wearily, his face etched with sorrow. "The circus came close, but the concert wasn't enough. We didn't draw them from the sky."

Harper felt as if her breath had been stolen from her. All that work, all that effort, all that wonderful music, and it still hadn't been enough.

The residents of the Tall Apartment Block rushed to her side and she felt their arms wrap around her. "It was a grand idea," whispered Great Aunt Sassy, embracing her. "You should be very proud of yourself."

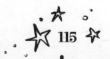

"It could have worked," said Isabella, wiping Harper's hair out of her eyes.

"There will be another way to find the circus," added Brigitte gently.

But Harper felt sadder than ever before. She missed the family she had only met in her dreams and she missed the hope of believing in the impossible.

Jack Willows came shuffling forward and put an instrument in Harper's hands. It was the small golden harp he had played in the concert. It looked a thousand years old. "I found this on the roof after the Fearsome Storm," said Jack kindly. "It's been in the lost property of the

Unforgotten Concert Hall ever since, but no one's ever claimed it. I think perhaps you should have it."

Harper didn't feel like playing anything. She wanted to snuggle up in bed and hide from the world, but at that moment, Faydra the fortune teller's words came back to her: "Play the instrument that calms the storm."

Harper sighed and wiped the dust from the harp's frame. She felt a tiny jolt of electricity flicker up her arm. She tried again and felt her heart leap softly as if she were somehow attached to the harp's strings. Then her fingers were moving and she was playing a familiar melody – a song she had never known how to play before,

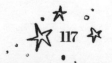

the song that haunted all of her dreams. The notes came easily now, without her thinking. She closed her eyes and almost didn't notice that the Scarlet Umbrella had picked up a breeze of its own accord and was carrying her into the Snowdrift clouds.

The song Harper played was simple and special. It felt like the tune that had been with her all of her life, like a story you speak without words. When the wind ceased, she found that the City of Clouds was far, far below her, and in front of her was the swirling red-and-gold tent of the circus. Only this time the tent was perfectly still.

Harper blinked and saw that all around the hovering tents a flock of birds were

fighting the pull of the wind. Fighting to hold the circus still. Fighting to give her time to reach her family. On the back of each bird was a storm-stirrer, and in the middle was the lightning-leader, keeping the storm at bay.

Skylar dived down on her white-winged eagle. "So it's you!" she laughed. "You're the little girl who escaped the circus."

Harper smiled. "I suppose I am."

"Keep playing your harp," Skylar called. "The song is an enchantment – it will bring your parents to you."

Harper felt the loveliness of the harp in her hands. As she began to play again, two black umbrellas came sailing towards her. Beneath them was a woman with

long locks and sea-grey eyes, and a man with storm-cloud hair. Harper held her breath. Suddenly she felt terribly shy. Midnight jumped from the top of the umbrella and curled around her shoulders. Bravely Harper looked up and saw that her parents' eyes were glistening with tears. Then she was crying too. In the air above the Tall Apartment Block in the City of Clouds, the three of them embraced as a family once again.

Chapter Thirteen
HARPER'S FAMILY

Aurelia spoke first, in a voice of sea salt and summer. "We love you so much, Harper. We were never supposed to be apart this long."

Hugo kissed the top of Harper's head. "We left you the harp and the Scarlet Umbrella, so that when you

played your song you could reach us."

Harper gave a big sudden sigh. So many things made sense to her in that moment. She pulled the note Sassy had saved for all these years from her pocket. "Oh," she said wistfully, "so that's the missing word in the note." And she read the sentence as it should be:

When the time is right, give her the Scarlet Umbrella and the Harp.

"So the harp was my true instrument all along." Harper smiled.

Hugo nodded. "It's the reason we named you Harper. We knew from when

you were very young that you had a rare musical gift."

"We wanted a musical name," added Aurelia. It was the nicest reason for a name Harper had ever known.

"But the Fearsome Storm must have snatched the harp away from you," Aurelia said sadly.

"Every biscuit I baked was harp-shaped and contained the notes of your song," Hugo explained.

"Every night I sang your tune and made it echo from the stars, hoping you would hear it," Aurelia breathed.

"I did hear it," Harper whispered. "It's the melody of my dreams. But I couldn't play it until I found the harp." Her parents'

faces were pale with sorrow, but their eyes were hopeful.

"Come with me," said Harper brightly. "Come and meet the people who've looked after me – the residents of the Tall Apartment Block."

The three of them floated down as softly as blossom to the crowd who stood ready to welcome them on the rooftop.

"Hugo! My darling boy, where an earth have you been?" cried Sassy, giving her nephew a huge hug, and planting a kiss on Aurelia's fair cheek.

"Thank you for taking care of our daughter," said Aurelia, wrapping Sassy in her long slender arms.

Harper held up the little old harp

proudly. "This is my true instrument," she announced. "It's the missing word from the note."

"And the reason for your name," smiled Hugo.

A hush of

astonishment swept across the rooftop. "Makes sense," Nate murmured to Ferdie, who nodded. "The answer was here in her name all along."

Liesel was silent. The sight of her friend with her parents, holding the harp, was all the proof she needed that fairy tales were real, and that one day one would find her.

"Oh, Harper, if only we'd known the missing word was 'harp'," gushed Great Aunt Sassy. "But at least you've found it now."

"So if the umbrella can fly, is the harp magical too?" asked Isabella.

Aurelia smiled and Nate, who was standing very close to her, could just make out the dazzle of her deep-sea beauty. "The harp is enchanted," Aurelia said. "But its spell

only works when Harper plays her song."
Everyone smiled in amazement. "When
she plays that one song Hugo and I will
come drifting from the clouds to wherever
she is."

Liesel's eyes were as wide as saucers.
"Will Harper live in the circus with you?"
she asked.

Hugo frowned heavily. "Not yet," he
said, touching his daughter's cheek and
turning to gaze at her. "Harper, in the
circus your musical gift would never be
allowed to shine. Othello Grande would
make you play piano until your nails were
wore thin, or have you teach the cello
to warthogs, or sing underwater like your
mother. There would be no freedom."

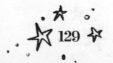

Harper listened and tried to understand. "So you wanted me to be free?" she asked.

Both her parents nodded. "If you do join the circus, we want it to be by choice, and not just because you were born into it," said Aurelia.

Hugo swept her into a hug and murmured, "Any time you need us, play the harp and we'll be here."

"Will we be able to come and visit you in the clouds?" asked Ferdie.

The Wild Conductor emerged from the crowd and answered, "No."

Everyone turned to stare at him and Hugo and Aurelia gave startled gasps. "Professor Armoury!" they uttered.

The Wild Conductor gave a sweeping

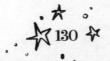

bow, and then continued explaining. "The Circus is bound by magic. You are either in or out. It's almost impossible to join, but even harder to leave." Hugo and Aurelia stared at their daughter glumly. "But in the summer when Othello Grande is away," the Wild Conductor said slyly, "then I might just be able to get you in – if you happen to have a flying umbrella." Harper's mind was suddenly alive with questions. There were so many things she wanted to ask. She grabbed her parents' hands and together they crept beneath the canopy of storm blooms, where the three of them talked until the moon was high.

Chapter Fourteen
A HAPPY FAREWELL

As Feather-fern clouds crossed the night sky, Peter and Brigitte arrived with hot cups of cocoa. Harper, Aurelia and Hugo came to join the other residents in the moonlight, and sip cocoa and falling rain.

"I guess we'll have to go soon," said

Aurelia gently. "The lightning-leader can't hold off the storm for ever."

Harper nodded and Hugo took her hand. "Before we go will you play us a song?" he asked.

Harper smiled and let her friends lead her to the little stage Nate's brothers had built. Ferdie, Nate and Liesel passed her their instruments and, as Midnight joined her on the mandolin, Harper began to juggle and play once again. This time everyone clapped and cheered as if their hearts might burst with love. Hugo and Aurelia could not have been prouder.

As Harper played the final note on her piccolo flute there was a whooshing of wings, and a girl who moved like lightning

leaped from the sky and landed on the rooftop.

"Skylar!" cried the children, gathering around her. Hugo and Aurelia both bowed to the storm-stirrer and the Wild Conductor tipped his hat.

"It's almost time to leave," said Skylar. "We can't hold the circus still for much longer."

"Harper, we wanted you to have this," said Aurelia, lifting a baby bird out of her pocket. It was a small pink dove, the very same one that had mistaken Liesel's hair as a nest.

"Her name is Storm," said Hugo. "If

you teach her your song, she'll be able to sing to Skylar's birds and send messages."

Skylar turned a happy somersault. "So we can keep in touch!" she laughed.

"Wait there," cried Harper, and she dashed into Elsie Caraham's little flat, where Memphis and Tallulah's kittens were soundly sleeping. All of them had homes to go to except one – a silver-and-black striped cat with sharp claws. At first glance she looked like a tabby. But if you knew cats the way they do in the City of Clouds, you would know that she was part Bengal – a hunter and adventurer.

Carefully, Harper picked up the sleeping kitten and carried it back to her parents. "She'll be pretty fierce, but the circus birds

are so huge that she would never be able to harm them," she said, handing them the little cat.

Skylar could not stop smiling. "A circus kitten!" she laughed. "The first cat to live in the clouds."

Aurelia covered her daughter's face with kisses. "We'll give her a name that reminds us of you – the girl with the Scarlet Umbrella."

"How about Ruby Mischief?" said Elsie Caraham, winking at Harper. Everyone chuckled – the name was right for the little cat in every way.

"We'd better get back to the circus," said Aurelia.

"Be brave, my little Harper" said Hugo, cuddling Harper closely.

The residents of the Tall Apartment Block stepped back as Harper hugged her parents goodbye. It was all so strange and new. But somehow it was OK. Harper stood with her feet firmly on the ground

and waved to the two dark umbrellas swinging away across the moon. Nate, Ferdie and Liesel stood beside her, waving to Harper's parents and their wonderful friend, the storm-stirrer.

Midnight slunk over to the man with the magpie-feather hair. Harper understood at once. She ran up to the Wild Conductor and threw her arms around him. "Thank you for helping me find my family," she said with a laugh. The Wild Conductor was so surprised, he almost toppled over.

"We'll help you get back into to the Circus of Dreams," Harper promised.

"And so will we," chorused her friends.

The Wild Conductor shrugged a little

awkwardly, gave a farewell bow, and then vanished down the stairwell and into the City of Clouds.

Harper yawned – she was incredibly tired. Nate took her hand and Smoke prowled beside her. Ferdie carried the Scarlet Umbrella and the harp. Liesel led the way, dancing back indoors with Storm the pink dove fluttering just in front, and Midnight came following three paces behind.

When they were all inside the little flat, Great Aunt Sassy fetched the birdcage from the bathroom. It had once held the Scarlet Umbrella, but now it made the perfect home for the small pink dove.

Harper wasn't sure she liked the idea of

birds in cages. "If I'm going to teach her my song, Storm will need to be happy," she said, opening the cage door. The little bird flew straight into Liesel's tangled hair and made a nest. "Maybe when we go on adventures, Storm could come too in your hair?" Liesel actually jumped for joy.

The wind whistled softly outside, a Summer-dew rain kissed the rooftop, and somewhere far off a clock chimed. It really was very late. The four children, the cat, the wolf and the little pink dove drew close and said goodnight. Then the poetic boy with the serious scarf and the small grubby girl who dreamed of dark forests skipped away down the stairs to floor five. And the boy who moved as softly as an

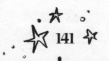

angel headed to floor ten, a silvery wolf at his side.

Then the girl with the rare musical gift curled up in bed, with her beloved Midnight purring beside her and Storm singing from her open cage.

She listened to the clicking of her fabulous Great Aunt Sassy's sewing machine and she knew in her heart that no matter how magical the circus was, the Tall Apartment Block in the City of Clouds was where she belonged.

Outside Harper's window the rain fell like a heartbeat and stars twinkled through a Feather-fern of cloud. Harper stroked the strings of the little harp. *At last I've found my true instrument,* she thought. *At*

last I can play my dream song. And at last I've found my family. She tucked the little Harp under her pillow, closed her eyes and fell into a deep, deep sleep.

Far away in the sky, in a circus tent, Hugo and Aurelia lay down to sleep. For the first time since the Fearsome Storm they were at peace. They had thought of Harper night after night, but when they did so now, she met them in their dreams and they sailed through the skies together, to the Circus of Dreams and beyond.

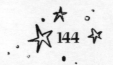

Also look out for . . .

HARPER
AND THE
Scarlet
Umbrella

Illustrated by Laura Ellen Anderson

When every single cat in the City of Clouds goes missing, Harper is determined to find her beloved Midnight and all the other precious pets.

Harper can't believe her luck when she discovers a magic flying umbrella and with the help of all her friends she sets off on a rescue adventure.

But they're up against the powerful Wild Conductor… Will they manage to bring the cats home?

Turn the page to read the beginning of this book.

Chapter One
THE BROKEN UMBRELLA

From the fourteenth floor of the Tall Apartment Block, Harper gazed dreamily across the City of Clouds. Trams rumbled through heavy rain and bright umbrellas bobbed like little boats.

"Darling, I'm leaving with the Dutch Opera House in ten minutes sharp," Great

Aunt Sassy cooed, as she stitched a pink petticoat into a gorgeous twirly gown. "They're picking me up by helicopter."

Harper smiled and put her arms around her Great Aunt Sassy's large waist, the

scent of lavender tickling her nose. Sassy Miller was the chief dressmaker for the Dutch Opera House. It was her job to sew hems, knit hats and create fabulous dresses.

Every four weeks, when the moon was round and full, Great Aunt Sassy travelled to Holland to check on all her beautiful gowns. Harper secretly liked it when Great Aunt Sassy went away, as she got to stay with the other residents of the Tall Apartment Block. Tonight she was staying with strange old Elsie Caraham, who lived on the topmost floor. Tomorrow she was with Madame Flora at the ballet school, on floor three.

Harper
AND THE
Sea of Secrets

This story was first published as a
World Book Day book in 2016.

This book is dedicated to anyone who struggles
with reading and writing. Dream big, fly high,
and never let anyone stop you.
Love, Cerrie
C.B.

For Charlie, my wonderful agent xxx
L.E.A.

First published in the UK in 2016 by Scholastic Children's Books
An imprint of Scholastic Ltd
Euston House, 24 Eversholt Street,
London, NW1 1DB, UK
Registered office: Westfield Road, Southam, Warwickshire, CV47 ORA
SCHOLASTIC and associated logos are trademarks and / or registered
trademarks of Scholastic Inc.

Text copyright © Cerrie Burnell, 2016
Illustrations copyright © Laura Ellen Anderson, 2016

The right of Cerrie Burnell to be identified as the author and
of Laura Ellen Anderson to be identified as the illustrator
has been asserted by them.

www.scholastic.co.uk

HARPER

AND THE

Sea of Secrets

CERRIE BURNELL

Illustrated by Laura Ellen Anderson

■SCHOLASTIC

Once there was a girl called Harper who had a rare musical gift. She heard songs on the wind, rhythms on the rain and hope in the beat of a butterfly's wing. Harper could play every instrument she touched, but her favourite of all was the harp. For whenever she played its silken strings, the air seemed to whisper with magic...

Chapter One

THE MESSENGER GULL

High on the topmost floor of the Tall
Apartment Block, Harper was dreaming
of music – a melody of stars and storms.
Suddenly, a frantic squawking cut through
the song, and her dream was full of feathers.

Harper opened a single sea-grey eye and
peered through a gap in the velvety curtains.
To her surprise a huge gull was hovering

outside. Its wings were the colour of the sea at dawn and its eyes were as sharp as flint. "You must have come from the sea," Harper breathed.

Elsie Caraham popped her head around the sitting-room door and gave a wild grin. "That, young Harper, is a messenger gull," she cried. "Look, it's carrying a message." Elsie Caraham was the oldest resident of the Tall Apartment Block. Harper was staying with her whilst her great aunt Sassy was away. If anyone knew anything about birds, it was Elsie, as she had lived near the skies all her life.

Harper seized her magical Scarlet Umbrella and ran out the door on to the rooftop, her pyjamas fluttering in the breeze. Exactly three paces behind her prowled Midnight, her beloved cat. In a matter of seconds, Harper

had flung the umbrella open, flipped it upside
down, hopped inside with Midnight and was
sailing up into the morning sky, towards the
circling gull.

In the stormy air above the City of Clouds, the gull dived towards the Scarlet Umbrella. Harper closed her eyes and shivered as the great bird rushed past, dropping the letter into her hands. Then, with a parting squawk, the gull was gone, soaring away to a far-off sea.

Harper's fingers trembled with excitement. She very rarely got letters, and when she did, it was normally birthday cards or poems from her friend Ferdie. But this letter looked different. For a start, the envelope was purple and it smelled faintly of lavender. "I think it's from Great Aunt Sassy!" Harper called down to Elsie who was watching from the rooftop as she tore the envelope open. Inside was a map, a set of directions and a note scrawled in lavender ink:

HELP!

The orchestra I'm working with have all had their instruments STOLEN!

You must bring new ones from the Tall Apartment Block to the City of Gulls at once!

Without instruments the SONGS OF THE SEA festival will be cancelled, and all my precious costumes will go to waste.

PLEASE HURRY!

Love,
Great Aunt Sassy
x

With the gentlest of thoughts, Harper brought the Scarlet Umbrella floating back to the rooftop. Before it had even landed, she pulled her piccolo flute from her pocket and played three sharp notes. This was the secret signal that let her three best friends know she needed their help.

Moments later, there was a scuffling sound at the far end of the rooftop. Harper, Midnight and Elsie stared as a small tangled ball of hair emerged from amongst some plant pots. The hair could well have been a nest for a family of mice, or it could have belonged to a child.

"Liesel!" Harper cried as a small bright-eyed girl with scuffed knees and a muddy face scampered up to her.

Next came a swish of sleek fur, and a wolf the shade of morning mist slunk on to the rooftop. At the wolf's side was a boy who moved as

silently as moonlight, and although he could hardly see the world around him, he knew every street of the city: Nate Nathanielson.

Lastly came Ferdie, a serious boy with a serious scarf and a pencil tucked behind his ear, ready to write down stories.

The four children, the wolf and the cat all crowded around the letter.

"Sassy needs our help," said Harper.

"There's only one thing for it," cried Ferdie. "We need to gather every instrument we can and tie them to the Scarlet Umbrella!"

Nate gave a wide grin. "Yes, just like we did when we rescued the cats from the Midnight Orchestra."

Liesel gave a twirl of glee, skipped across the roof and rang a large silver bell. This was the Tall Apartment Block's meeting bell, which summoned every resident to the rooftop.

Within minutes a crowd had gathered. As soon as they heard the news of the stolen instruments they stumbled off sleepily, still in their dressing gowns, and returned with a splendid collection.

There was a huge and mighty double bass, a round, booming drum, a sparkling trombone, Madame Flora's cherry-wood piano, Harper's precious cello, Ferdie's button accordion, Liesel's silver triangle and Nate's brother's Roman tuba!

Elsie Caraham and Madame Flora took a strand of edentwine – an unbreakable string made from the stems of storm blooms – and set to work tying each instrument to the handle of the Scarlet Umbrella. Nate carefully attached a large kite and Midnight's cat basket. Ferdie took hold of the kite like a glider, and Liesel shot into the cat basket.

166

Harper scooped up Midnight, leaped into the upside-down umbrella, and helped Nate in after her. With a wondrous bound Smoke joined them, her golden eyes blazing like stars.

"Good luck," Elsie cheered, waving them off. Harper closed her eyes and, with a silent wish, commanded the Scarlet Umbrella to take them into the sky. Up they soared, up high above the City of Clouds, four children, a cat, a wolf and a trail of magnificent instruments, gleaming in the morning rain.

They were on their way to City of Gulls. They were on their way to adventure.

Chapter Two

THE CITY OF GULLS

"Follow the river north!" yelled Ferdie, studying the map in his hands.

"Got it," called Nate, reaching out over the side of the Scarlet Umbrella and feeling through cloudburst rain and a patch of thunder.

Liesel peered down from the cat basket and gave a scream of excitement when the

river roared into view.

"Which way now?" asked Harper.

"Follow the river to the foot of the Mist Mountain, then turn left and pick up the scent of the sea," cried Ferdie.

"OK," Harper smiled. As the peak of Mist Mountain loomed into sight, she helped Nate steer the Scarlet Umbrella left, then whispered to it, "Take us to the sea." At once, the sharp scent of salt tickled their noses. Then the clouds thinned and the children gasped.

You see, in the City of Clouds there are six types of rain that fall, float and patter from the sky every single day, in many different ways. Rain is what the children knew, and rain was the weather they loved the best. But as the Scarlet Umbrella carried them far from home, they were each struck by golden-bright sunshine. Harper laughed in

amazement, and Ferdie quickly loosened his scarf. He much preferred cold, lonely greyness.

Nate smiled and took off his hat, and Liesel leaped and turned a perfect pirouette in the cat basket.

A wild sea-wind snatched up the Scarlet Umbrella as if it were a fallen leaf. The children whooped and clung on tightly as they soared towards the City of Gulls, the instruments clanging and banging and sending odd notes of music tumbling down into the day.

"The City Gulls!" Liesel squealed as thousands of soaring birds came into sight." But it was not just gulls that swooped through the sky. Seabirds of every type were circling the green waters, their wings spread wide, their eyes seeking out silvery fish.

Smoke sat up straight, her nose tipped

towards where the moon might be, howling with happiness and hope. Nate laughed and ruffled her fur.

Harper noticed that the city itself was a peculiar little place, full of winding lanes and quaint old shops selling ships in bottles or deep-sea treasures. Instead of thick cloud the air was full of light, and the cry of the gulls rang through the streets.

She shivered with excitement. There was definitely a sense of mystery to this place.

Above her, Ferdie peered down from his kite. "The rooftops here look haunted," he murmured, deciding at once that he liked City of Gulls very much. It looked like the kind of place old explorers might live in. Ferdie pulled his pencil from behind his ear and began scribbling a sea-shanty.

"Look, there's an old crumbling pier," said

Liesel, quickly describing it for Nate. "It's a strange old structure that's half fallen into the sea."

"There's no sand on the beach," added Harper, "just a shore of pale white pebbles and sea of swirling green."

Nate listened happily. He could make out the dazzling glitter of the water, like a shadow edged in starlight, and he could feel the kiss of salt on his skin.

As they swooped down over the beach, they saw a bandstand and the Royal Seaside Pavilion. Gathered upon the bandstand was an orchestra of musicians without a single instrument, all miming the notes they should have been playing.

"What are they doing?" asked Ferdie.

"Pretending to play imaginary instruments," said Harper sadly.

"Perhaps they'll cheer up now we've brought them some real ones," Nate grinned. But he could not have been more wrong. For no sooner had Great Aunt Sassy come running out of the Seaside Pavilion and carefully helped the children lower each instrument on to the bandstand, than the entire orchestra started moaning. And what a terrible fuss they made! Harper had never heard such a racket.

"We can't possibly play this drum, it's not loud enough!" huffed a large ruby-cheeked man whose voice seemed to boom.

"And I simply cannot play this cello, it's too old," declared a graceful woman with curvy dark hair.

"This double bass is not acceptable," piped up a tall man with sturdy shoulders.

"Well, this piano is out of tune," complained

a red-haired woman with a fretful frown.

Liesel scowled at the woman crossly. "Perhaps you just don't know how to play it," she said, with a toss of her messy curls.

The orchestra glared at the small girl angrily, their eighty pairs of eyes staring hard. Ferdie stood up taller – he was ready to stick up for his sister. Great Aunt Sassy flapped her arms anxiously, and turned round and round like a confused duck.

Smoke gave a low forewarning growl and the orchestra all took a huge step back. At once Nate's hand was on the wolf's head, soothing her mood. That was the wonderful thing about Smoke: she wasn't wild, but nor was she tame. Her heart was filled with loyalty for Nate. Yet with time, Smoke had grown very fond of Nate's friends – especially light-footed Liesel.

Nate softly stepped forward. "Listen," he said calmly to the orchestra. "There's no need to get upset. We just wanted to help with Songs of the Sea Festival. If you won't play the music, then Harper could instead." Nate turned his face towards his friend and beamed. For although he couldn't see her, he saw the outline of a girl who shimmered with harmonies, and he winked, making Harper smile.

Midnight tiptoed over to the cherry-wood piano and began tuning the notes with his tail. The orchestra stared with astonishment as Harper kissed Midnight's nose, then sat down to play. Each ivory key she touched seemed to fill the air with tunes that echoed of water and waves.

She moved on to the cello, followed by the double bass, drum and then the glistening trombone, with which she played three sharp notes. The others knew what to do. Ferdie began squeezing the button accordion, Liesel let the silver triangle ring out and Nate went wild on the Roman tuba, whilst Midnight and Smoke played a duet on Harper's cello.

By the end of the performance, the orchestra all looked quite sheepish. They muttered an apology and quickly went

back to miming the notes. Harper sighed. "They're still cross they've lost their own instruments."

"Well," said Ferdie in a serious tone, "unless we want to put up with more bad moods, we better try and find the missing instruments."

The others all gave a nod.

"Yes," agreed Nate, "let's split up."

Chapter Three
THE SMUGGLERS' MAP

Harper and Ferdie set off into the heart of the City of Gulls at a run. The city felt as odd as it had looked. Everything was slightly crooked, so neither of them could tell if they were walking up a hill or stumbling down a ditch.

Midnight, who normally tiptoed three paces behind Harper, scampered lightly in

front and darted through the doorway of a higgledy-piggledy shop. It was called "The Pirate's Pearl". The two children rushed after Midnight, but the little shop was packed so full of junk they had to climb over a massive barrel of rum and crawl beneath a three-legged table just to get inside.

Midnight sprang on to an old oak cabinet, knocking over a long wooden tube with a swish of his white-tipped tail. "Watch out," cried Ferdie, leaping to catch it.

The lid of the tube popped open and a faded sheet of parchment slipped to the floor. "What is it?" asked Harper as Ferdie carefully unfolded it.

"It's a map of underground passageways," Ferdie grinned, "all leading to the same place: Gull Island."

"What's Gull Island?" asked Harper.

"It's an old smuggler's hideout, just off the coast," echoed a voice croaky with sleep.

Harper and Ferdie spun around to see an old man sitting in a rocking chair. His eyebrows were snow-coloured, and he looked like he'd been snoozing for the last hundred years.

The old man winked a bright blue eye and gave a big crinkly smile before stumbling to his feet and saying in grand voice, "Ahoy, there! I'm Slim Joe, owner of the Pirate's Pearl and expert on the City of Gulls. What can I do for you?"

"We're looking for stolen instruments," said Ferdie.

Slim Joe gave a wise chuckle. "This city is built upon secrets," he said mysteriously.

Harper smiled. She knew there was something special about this place, and she could feel it under her feet.

"It's a smugglers' town, you see," Slim Joe went on. "Beneath the streets is indeed a maze of tunnels that lead out under the sea."

Both children gave a gasp of delight.

"Of course nobody uses the tunnels any more," said Slim Joe, pouring three cups of tea from a rusty old kettle.

"Why not?" asked Harper.

"Nobody knows the way in," Slim Joe shrugged.

"But doesn't it say on the map?" asked Ferdie.

Slim Joe shook his head. "The map marks all the tunnels, but it got torn, and now no one knows where the entrance is."

Ferdie gulped down a swig of bitter tea.

"We'll take the map," he cried, tightening his scarf.

"Consider it a gift," beamed Slim Joe.

"I wonder what other secrets this town holds," said Harper quietly.

"Well, plenty of folk say they hear songs coming from the waves. It's not called Sea of Secrets for nothing," mumbled Slim Joe.

Harper's eyes widened. "Come on," she cried, "we've got to get back to the beach."

Slim Joe watched in stunned silence as the two children ran into the street, scooped up Midnight, opened the Scarlet Umbrella and raced into the air. Soon their feet were skimming the rooftops as they flew through soaring gulls.

On the stony shores of the Sea of Secrets, Liesel and Nate wandered towards the

crumbling pier. Liesel danced ahead, her feet hardly touching the stones. Nate took in every crunch of every pebble, every fizz of every wave, every screech of every gull that looped the sky.

He loved it, and so did Smoke. There was a wildness in her step that Nate had only known her use at night. She was a blur of mist, a shadow with a heartbeat, streaking in and out of the waves, her fur turned silver with salt.

Then the wolf stopped, her ears pricked. She was picking up a sound that Nate couldn't hear. Liesel, who knew Smoke well, scurried over.

"Can you see anything strange?" asked Nate.

Liesel scanned the horizon, her small eyes beady as a gull's. "There's nothing but a boat

full of fishermen," she shrugged.

"Oh," smiled Nate. "Maybe Smoke can hear them singing." For the fishermen were all singing a lullaby of some sort.

But, as Liesel watched the beautiful wolf, she noticed Smoke was staring at the waves beyond. "Wait," she said, yanking Nate's sleeve. "I think Smoke's listening to something in the sea."

The children froze as, ever so faintly, the sound of music came drifting up from the pale green waves.

Chapter Four

THE BOAT OF BEARDY FISHERMEN

It didn't take Liesel long to find an abandoned rowing boat. With a wild splash and a nudge from Smoke, she got the boat into the water. Nate, who had never been in a boat before, clambered in and grabbed the two wooden oars in the bottom. With the wolf yapping at his side and Liesel sitting at the front, he began to steadily row. Soon they were out of icy shallows and close to the boat of beardy

fishermen. But the fishermen weren't taking any notice. Nate wasn't going to stand for his friend being ignored. He raised the Roman tuba to his lips and blew it like a foghorn.

The fishermen leaped like startled frogs. One fell into a bucket of eels, one almost toppled overboard, whilst another clung to the boat's white sail in terror. Then they spotted the two children and scowled. Nate couldn't see the fishermen clearly, but he could tell that they were men who had very big beards and that they moved as quickly as cats.

"We heard songs coming from the sea," Liesel yelled.

"Nothing to do with us, Miss," grumbled a fisherman with a telescope.

"They say the seas are haunted," chimed in another, who was holding a pipe.

"Might be your imagination," mumbled a third with a lot of tattoos.

Liesel frowned fiercely. "Wait here," she whispered to Nate, and before anyone could stop her, she sprang from the rowing boat and landed aboard the fishermen's boat. Nate laughed as he realized what was happening and Liesel began to climb the sail, her

heart beating fast with joy. The fishermen cried out in anger, shaking their fists and bellowing. Though they were quick as cats, Liesel was quick as a mouse, and she reached the top of the mast in no time. You see, Liesel was a girl who dreamed of dancing with pirates and swimming with sharp-finned sharks. This beardy band of fishermen didn't scare her at all.

From the top of the sail she spotted a young boy who wasn't much older than Nate, and she beckoned to him. The boy, whose hair was fiery red, climbed the sail and, when no one was watching, he whispered to Liesel, "Take no notice of them."

"I won't," she grinned. "My name's Liesel. Who are you?"

"Samson," replied the boy. "This is my mum's boat, I keep an eye on it for her while

she's selling fish at the market." Then he added secretively, "These waters are wild and the sea is full of strange sounds."

Liesel's eyes twinkled. "So we *did* hear music!"

The boy nodded, and then stared down at the shore and frowned. Leisel quickly followed his gaze, and for a moment she thought she saw a woman at the end of the pier, with sunset hair and a beautiful cello. "You know, you might want to get off the boat before we dock," said Samson hurriedly. "Why?" asked Liesel. Samson shrugged and fidgeted. "It's just my mum might get

192

cross if she finds out I let you on to the boat."

"Is that your mum?" asked Liesel, pointing back to the shore — but the woman and the cello had disappeared. She pulled a tuneless recorder from her pocket and played three sharp notes. There was a faint whooshing sound, and Samson gasped as an umbrella of stunning scarlet silk descended from the clouds.

"Grab on," Ferdie yelled, reaching out to his sister. With a quick wave to Samson and the speechless fisherman below, Liesel leaped into her brother's arms, and away they all soared back to the beach, sweeping up Nate and Smoke as they went.

The tide was going out fast and, as they reached the pebbles, the children noticed that all along the crumbling pier children were perched with fishing lines, happily catching

crabs. Nate had never touched a crab before. Ferdie stayed with Smoke so she didn't munch all the bait. Harper led Nate up on to the pier and Midnight reached out a long claw, plucking a small red crab from a bucket for Nate.

Liesel did what a mouse might do: she darted and scampered along the pier until she reached the very end, where she crouched down low and gazed at the lapping sea. There below her, wading through the water, was Samson, the fiery-haired boy from the boat.

Liesel was about to call out when a seagull swooped from the air, trying to peck a piece of bacon. Liesel shooed it away. When she looked back, Samson was gone. Nowhere to be seen. He seemed to have vanished into the soft sea air.

Chapter Five

A LULLABY OF LOST SHIPS

Twilight fell across the City of Gulls and the sea turned fish-scale grey. "It's odd that everyone here is so grumpy," said Nate as they wandered back to the Seaside Pavilion.

"But not Slim Joe!" beamed Ferdie, pulling out the piece of parchment and showing it to his friends. "It's a map of all the tunnels

below the city. They all lead to the same place: Gull Island."

"Wow," breathed Nate, feeling the edges. He could always tell how old a note or letter was by the amount of creases that crossed it. This map was very old indeed.

Just then Great Aunt Sassy came tearing out of the doors of the Seaside Pavilion. "Harper, there you are, my love!" she cooed, giving her a warm hug. "Do go inside — we're in room seven. There are plenty of beds for all."

The children gazed at the bundle of splendid costumes billowing in Sassy's arms. "These precious outfits are for the festival — if we can find the instruments," Sassy sighed. Harper spotted a bright blue scarf, Liesel eyed a wondrous purple cloak, Ferdie admired a rather stylish tweed jacket and Nate felt the whisper of velvet.

"Well, I'd better deliver them to the orchestra just the same," Sassy smiled. With a swish of lavender silk, she was gone, sweeping down the stairs and into the evening mist.

The children dashed inside and found

room seven, which was indeed full of beds! There was a bunk bed, a queen's bed, a sofa bed, a hammock, a basket, a camp bed and a very bouncy waterbed. The most remarkable thing about the waterbed was that curled up happily in the middle of it was Midnight!

How he got into the room, or knew which bed Harper might choose, was a mystery. You see, Midnight was a most unusual cat. He seemed to know more about Harper than she did herself, sometimes prowling three steps behind, other times appearing at the very place she was supposed to be.

Harper curled up next to him, stroking his nightshade fur. "You're my best friend," she whispered.

Ferdie swung from the bunk to the sofa, before deciding the hammock was the perfect poet's nest. Liesel at once curled up in the

basket, much like a tired little mouse. Nate and Smoke settled eagerly down in the camp bed, the wolf becoming a pillow of claws and tail.

The moon cast bold shadows, and the children, the cat and the wolf drifted into a deep and wondrous slumber.

In her dream, Harper was lying upon the double bass, plucking its fine strings as it floated out to sea. All around her, stars reflected on the surf, dancing and glimmering to the tune she played: a shanty of salt and sorrows that whispered of wonder and waves.

Then suddenly there was howling and meowing, and someone was shaking her awake. "Harper, the sea is singing!" Ferdie cried.

Harper blinked her tired eyes and found that she wasn't playing the double bass

or sailing out to sea. She was lying on the waterbed, and the glorious song from her dream was echoing up from the beach.

Smoke and Midnight led the way out of their room and down to the beach where the children gathered listening to a song as mysterious as the moon that shimmered on the far-off waves. "If only we could reach the sea," sighed Harper.

Nate sniffed the dry salty air and shook his head. "Tide's too far out," he said.

"And it's too dark to see anything," Ferdie frowned.

"Not if you have these," came a voice through the moonlight.

The children turned to see Great Aunt Sassy leaning dramatically against the cherry-wood piano, clutching an armful of tiny lanterns, which flickered like fairy lights.

Around her were all the instruments they had brought from the Tall Apartment Block. At once Harper knew what they needed to do. "Grab an instrument," she cried, "Great Aunt Sassy, follow me to the sea!"

A little while later, Harper and Midnight were sitting in the Scarlet Umbrella, gently guiding it across silver-bright waves, towing her friends behind in a procession of music and love.

First came Ferdie, Nate and golden-eyed Smoke, riding upon the double bass. Next bobbed Liesel, tucked perfectly into the end of an upturned French horn. Lastly came Great Aunt Sassy, squashed inside a bass drum, her lavender petticoats billowing in the breeze.

Water lapped softly around them, strings twanged and the children giggled. Then the

song of the sea took hold of them and no one dared speak.

The music was just like in Harper's dream: a lullaby of lost ships with murmurs of mermaids.

For Ferdie, it was poetry. He grabbed his pencil and began scrawling words to sing to the tune.

For Liesel, it was energy, a tug at her toes that she couldn't ignore. She rose out of the French horn and twirled around upon its edge, like a marvellous midnight flamingo.

For Nate, it was stillness and beauty, a splendour that gripped him with joy.

For Sassy, it was a dream of costumes yet to come.

And for Harper, the melody was many things, but most of all it was love. She leaned over the edge of the Scarlet Umbrella, trying

to follow the sound, and gasped. "It's not just music," she breathed. "There are lights too."

The others peered down into the darkening sea and felt their hearts leap. Deep beneath the surface, glowing flecks of light flared like fallen stars. "It's like a rainbow at the bottom of the ocean," Ferdie whispered.

Nate smiled, for though he couldn't see the lights, he could sense his friends' amazement. "Where do you think it's coming from?" he whispered back.

Ferdie pulled the map of the smugglers' tunnels from his pocket and studied it by moonlight. "Perhaps someone is smuggling the instruments to Gull Island," he yelled.

They all stared through the dark in the direction of Gull Island, and sure enough, there in the distance, like stars shrouded in mist, was a light.

206

"Let's go there now," cried Harper, but Great Aunt Sassy softly cleared her throat.

"Darlings, it's awfully late and simply too far to sail to."

The children, who were shivering and actually couldn't stop yawning, knew deep down that Sassy was right. "If only we knew where the entrance to the tunnels was," Ferdie sighed crossly.

Liesel sat very still in her trombone. She thought of Samson, and how he seemed to have vanished into the sea. In the glow of the moon, she smiled. If anyone was mischievous enough to find a secret door, she was.

"Leave it to me," she chuckled.

Chapter Six

THE SECRET TUNNEL

When the soft pink light of dawn spread across the City of Gulls, Liesel was already awake. In fact, she was boinging up and down between the different beds, trying to get everyone's attention. "Come on, come on – I've found the entrance to the smugglers' tunnel!"

This got everybody out of bed pretty quickly – apart from Great Aunt Sassy, who

was wrapped in a shroud of sheets, snoring loudly.

The children crept outside, then ran like the wind to the crumbling pier. "How did you find it?" called Harper.

"I snuck out with Smoke and Midnight as soon as the sun rose and discovered it behind a rock," Liesel said, plunging knee-deep into icy water and wading to the end of the pier.

The others followed and, sure enough, cut into the rock behind a thick clump of black seaweed, was a door.

"Ta-dah!" Liesel yelled, jumping almost as high as the pier. She tried to wrench it open, and her face fell. It was locked.

Harper fumbled in her pocket and pulled out a hairpin. She handed it to Nate with a hopeful grin. "Will this do?"

Nate, who could open any door without

a key, set about trying to pick the lock. But the pin snapped. The lock wouldn't budge. "I need something bigger, something sharper," he mumbled.

Without any warning, Midnight leaped out of Harper's arms and swiped something red from the cold water. It was the shell of lobster claw.

"Good boy," beamed Nate as he slotted the claw carefully into the lock. With a loud groaning sound, the lock popped open and the door swung wide.

"Everyone inside," yelled Ferdie, and once they were all safely through the door, he yanked it shut behind them.

Suddenly the children were in utter blackness — somewhere very damp that smelled of rust and fishbones. For a moment Midnight's eyes held the light of the sun,

showing the children they were in a small leaky tunnel.

Then Midnight blinked and they were in darkness once again. But the children were not afraid. They knew that Nate was a boy of many talents, and one of them was that he could walk through the darkness just as easily as if it was day.

"Hold hands," he said gently, shuffling to the front of the line. Smoke walked proudly at her master's side while Nate guided the others further into the dark. Then boy and wolf stopped still. "The tunnel splits into two," said Nate. "Which one should we take?"

Nobody knew what to do. Harper closed her eyes and thought hard, and that was when she heard a sound. Not a loud sound, nor a long sound, but a sound that was full of light.

It was a single note played on the instrument Harper knew best.

"This way," she said, stumbling forwards and leading her friends to the left, for she was certain that at the end of the tunnel, someone was playing the harp. And she was right.

The four salt-skinned children, the cat and the wolf burst from the tunnel on to a beach of golden sand in a hidden cove on Gull Island.

Smoke gave an angry snarl, her fur standing up on end. Midnight leaped on to Harper's shoulders and the children stopped still. In front of them stood a bunch of beardy fishermen, each clutching an instrument like a weapon of war.

Harper stepped forward and gave them a smile. "I think you might have something that belongs to the orchestra," she said coolly.

Chaos broke out and the fishermen all

213

started shouting and stamping, but Harper held their gaze. You see, she had had to face other musicians far more terrifying than this seafaring band.

"Well, finders keepers. They're ours now," jeered the fisherman with the pipe.

"But why do you need them?" cried Ferdie.

"Do you know how to play?" added Nate.

The fishermen fidgeted uncomfortably, then from the middle of them stepped a woman with fiery red hair. She was as fierce and as beautiful as a storm at sea.

"Who are you?" spluttered Ferdie, who was in secret awe of this pirate-like woman.

Liesel stared at the woman's fiery hair and knew exactly who she was. "You're Samson's mum, aren't you?" she smiled.

The woman's face softened, "I am, lassie. My name's Una."

"Well, can you please tell us what's going on?" demanded Liesel.

Una, to everyone's surprise, said nothing. Instead, she picked up a fiddle and began to merrily play. She did not play it gracefully, or smoothly, or softly. She played it as if her soul was on fire, leaping around like a wild bird. The sound she made was astonishing.

Harper held her breath, and as the tune danced into her heart, she thought of the orchestra and their fabulous costumes. Then she pictured the grumpy fishermen who spent every day at sea, learning lullabies of lost ships and the wonders of the waves, and all at once she understood. She opened her eyes and spoke. "You are the ones who know the real *Songs of the Sea,* aren't you?"

The fishermen nodded solemnly.

"That's right, lassie," said Una. "We all play an instrument of some sort — be it a drum or crab basket. And we're right fed up of the orchestra taking over our festival."

Ferdie stood up straighter. He was a serious boy with a serious scarf, and he'd just had a seriously good idea. "What if we lent you some other instruments?" he suggested. "Then would you give these ones back?"

There was a lot of muttering and whispering. "How many instruments you got?" asked the fisherman with the telescope.

"Not enough," said Nate, listening to the many mumbling voices.

"I could always play my clam-organ," came a small voice from the back.

Everyone turned to see a boy with the same flame-red hair as Una holding up a set of clam-shells. "Samson!" Liesel grinned.

With a swift wink from Una, Samson started playing the clams like a mini mouth organ. The sound was shrill and funny, like the rushing of water over stones. It gave Harper a wonderful idea. She picked up a large pink shell and blew it like a horn. "If we could find enough shells I could teach you how to be the first-ever seashell band!"

Chapter Seven

THE SONGS OF THE SEA FESTIVAL

Almost at once a collection of seashells appeared on the golden sand. There was a huge grey shell almost bigger than Liesel that Samson and Ferdie strung fishing wire across, turning it into a cello – or *shello*.

There was a bundle of mussel shells which could be played like a glockenspiel. There were larger shells that formed fishing-wire

fiddles and a chorus of conches that could be played like flutes.

Harper found the fishermen were all excellent learners, and they knew the songs of the sea by heart. When the sun cast midday shadows, the band of beards were ready for the festival.

"Was it you playing last night in the tunnels below the sea?" asked Nate as they boarded the boat to sail back to the City of Gulls. The fishermen all chuckled and shook their heads.

"No," said the man covered in tattoos. "Nobody knows who plays those strange songs."

Liesel, who was perched at the top of the sail with Samson, gazed at the sea. It was as still as ice. Then, just for a second, she saw the surface break, and something strange and

mythical rose out of the water. "I saw a sea dragon!" she gasped.

Everyone ran to the edge of the boat. Ferdie seized a telescope and squinted through the lens, then almost dropped it in surprise. "Wow," he stuttered. "It's not a sea dragon … it's a whale."

Una shook her head. "There aren't any such beasts in these waters any more."

But her son Samson spoke up. "There are, Mum. They've come back. I see them sometimes when I'm night fishing. There are dolphins, too. They're pretty shy, but if you play music, they come closer."

The fishermen all turned to stare at Harper, their eyes now twinkling with hope.

"Would you play something, lass?" asked Una.

Harper's face lit up in a smile. With the

help of Ferdie and Nate, she opened the Scarlet Umbrella, lowered it over the edge of the boat and stepped in. From deep within the umbrella's folds, Harper pulled a small, very old golden harp and started to softly play.

Her fingers found the notes of the tune from her dream: a harmony of sailors' hearts all singing their love to the seas.

Ever so slowly, all around her, the surf began to glow. At first, there was just a glimpse of dazzling turquoise, then a flash of bright jade, followed by bursts of pink and orange. A chorus of tails broke the surface, and shooting air rose from the waves.

"The whales are coming!" Liesel gasped. And they were. A school of legend-like mammals made a ring around the Scarlet Umbrella.

Harper kept playing as more and more sea

creatures came to join the song. There were bright-eyed dolphins and grey-skinned seals, glittering starfish and an inky octopus.

Harper stood up, with Midnight prowling elegantly along the rim of the umbrella. "Right," she called to the fishermen, "who's ready to put on a show?"

When three o'clock came in the City of Gulls, the orchestra's instruments had been returned to the bandstand, much to their great relief. The musicians all looked fantastic in Great Aunt Sassy's gorgeous gowns.

Amongst the cheerful audience sat Ferdie, Liesel and Nate, each of them giddy with excitement.

Smoke pricked her ears as the orchestra began to play. It was a stunning performance,

made up of tender melodies and tunes of moondust.

Just as the show came to an end, a new sound reached everyone's ears: the sound of a girl playing a solo on a strange old harp in the middle of the sea. Colours began flickering under the water, and a harmony echoed up from the waves.

Then there came a clapping of clamshells and a banging of baskets as a boat with white sails floated into view. On board, the band of beards raised their shells into the air and began to play for all they were worth – songs of patch-eyed pirates and shanties of sharp-toothed sharks.

The audience were spellbound. As Harper played on, gulls began to swarm in time to the beat, and the orchestra, enchanted by happiness, grabbed bows and horns and joined in.

The bandstand, the waters and the skies were alive with songs of the seas, all of them following the girl with the harp. The three children and Great Aunt Sassy could not have been prouder. Ferdie leaped up and grabbed the button accordion. Liesel joined in on the triangle, and Nate tooted away on the Roman tuba as if he'd been born on a boat.

It was the best Songs of the Sea Festival the City of Gulls had ever known. The fishermen, the orchestra and everyone in the town could finally be friends.

Later that evening, when the sun had set into the Sea of Secrets and the whales and sea creatures had all swum away, diving down deep to a world of blue, Una put her arms around Harper and thanked her. "You rescued the festival and made it what it should have always been," she said gently.

Harper smiled, "It wasn't just me. I couldn't have done it without my friends – or without Samson."

Una ruffled each of the children's sand-filled hair. "You're welcome to sail with us any time," she beamed.

Liesel's eyes lit up like sparklers and Ferdie had to hold her hand to stop her jumping aboard the boat right away. Nate gave a sailor's salute and, through the first rays of twilight, he could just make out a band of beardy fishermen grandly saluting back.

The children waved, Smoke howled, Midnight mewed a proud meow, and Samson called goodbye, then the boat with white sails was gone.

Great Aunt Sassy threw her arms around the four children. "You really saved the day!" she gushed, and because she was in a very

good mood, she added, "Shall we go out on the sea once more to hear the whales sing?" The children glowed with joy.

So the instruments were strung together and the girl with a harp towed out her friends in her enchanted umbrella. Behind her, the boy who knew the dark like the day smiled at his wolf. Beside him, on the double bass, a boy with a poet's heart pulled his pencil from behind his ear and got ready to write. And a little way off, a girl who dreamed of dancing with pirates imagined herself on a sea-bound adventure.

Great Aunt Sassy gazed up at the silver stars. Tomorrow they would travel back to the City of Clouds, but tonight was all about the sea. As it lapped softly around the instruments, the waters began to sparkle and the whale song began.

The children bobbed closer together and held hands. Far off on the midnight waters, like a ghost beneath the moon, sailed a ship with white sails, clanging out the songs of the sea upon shells. The children laughed — the band of beards was playing again.

"I hope we come back here," yawned Liesel, as they headed back to shore.

"We should come on a hot summer's day," smiled Nate, who was really rather tired.

"Then we could swim and join the dolphins," grinned Ferdie.

"And sing with the whales," sighed Harper, her eyes beginning to close.

Even though they had the choice of many lovely beds up at the Pavilion, the children decided to sleep on the bandstand, curled up on their instruments, gazing out at the starry sea.

"Sweet dreams, Midnight," Harper whispered, snuggling down beneath the Scarlet Umbrella, and listening to the lull of the waves. Midnight winked a green eye at her and twitched his ears. He took a last look at the glittering water and nestled under Harper's chin.

In her dreams, Harper was sailing in a boat with sails of scarlet silk, playing a small golden harp. From the waves she heard music — a song as old as time and wise as oceans — and she knew that one day they would all come back and learn more of the secrets of the sea.

Cerrie Burnell is a presenter and writer, best known for her work in children's TV, and she featured in the *Guardian*'s 2011 list of 100 most inspirational women. Her other titles in this same series include *Harper and the Scarlet Umbrella* and *Harper and the Night Forest* (publishing in March 2017).

Laura Ellen Anderson is the incredibly talented illustrator of the *John Smith Is Not Boring* series and The *Witch Wars* series, as well as all the other *Harper* titles.

Picture books by the same creators: